FUN STORIES

FOR YOUR DRIVE HOME

R. SCOTT MURPHY

Dedicated to Jenny, Jordan, Griffin, Curly, Mom, Dad, Jennifer, and—the greatest storyteller of all-time—Casey Kasem.

For the good folks of Austin, Texas

For Professor McConaughey (Minister of Culture)

Tom Petty, we love and miss you. Thanks for providing so many contributions to the soundtrack of my life.

ALRIGHT, ALRIGHT, ALRIGHT!

END OF WORK WHISTLE

*C*ongratulations, you did it! Your workday is over! It's now time to flip the script and have some fun. A good way to shift into Fun Mode is to say the catchphrase actor Matthew McConaughey made famous when he played the character David Wooderson in the coming-of-age comedy *Dazed and Confused*. It goes, "Alright, alright, alright!"

The phrase washes away all the bad parts from your workday and helps you find your chill. It's even more fun if you imitate McConaughey's character from the movie when you say, "Alright, alright, alright!" Sometimes, on Fridays, I say it a dozen or more times as I drive out of my work parking lot.

Fun fact: The scene where McConaughey says, "Alright, alright, alright!" was the first scene he ever shot in his acting career. In fact, he wasn't even supposed to be in the scene. It took place outside a famous Austin, Texas fast-food restaurant called Top Notch *(check it out the next time you are in the ATX).*

As he set the scene, director Richard Linklater felt like McConaughey's character would be the kind of person that would hang out at Top Notch. Linklater told McConaughey he'd like him to make an appearance in the scene even though it wasn't in the script.

McConaughey agreed to give it a try. He took a 30-minute walk to get a feel of how his character related to the scene. McConaughey asked himself, "What is David Wooderson all about?" He then decided that his character was about at least three things: his car, his rock 'n' roll music, and his pursuit of girls.

When he later entered the scene, McConaughey realized he could check off all three boxes. He was in his car; he was listening to rock music, and he was about to talk to a red-haired girl. In character, McConaughey confidently blurted out, "Alright, alright, alright!"

The phrase stuck with him. At the 86th Academy Awards, when he won the best actor award for *Dallas Buyers Club*, McConaughey stepped up to the microphone and said, "Alright, alright, alright!"

It's a phrase that helps you get into Fun Mode and prepares you for adventure. Speaking of fun adventures, I'd like to thank you for joining me for another *Fun Stories* book adventure. You can read this book in any place, at any time; but to add to the fun, I am presupposing that you are enjoying this book at the end of your workday.

Think of me as part storyteller, part game-show host, part DJ, and part madcap tour guide. I'm about to share some crazy stories about work, school, home, dating, and much more. No topic is off-limits as I seek to help you check off the boxes you need checked-off in order to have fun. You'll also be surprised by how often I can get myself into awkward and embarrassing situations.

Before the book is over, I'm going to quit the Cub Scouts, wear a police helmet backward, create an ugly scene at a soccer game for four-year-olds, witness the ultimate waitress revenge, watch my new employee mentor misbehave, and hand out a Clown Commuter Award.

It all begins right here, right now. Say it with me as you turn the page, "Alright, alright, alright!"

Hear the iTunes/Apple Music Version

CUB SCOUT DROPOUT

*O*ur family recently attended an Eagle Scout ceremony for the youngest son of our friends—The Malones. Both their sons are Eagle Scouts, and the Dad, Todd, is also an Eagle Scout. That's really impressive stuff.

Shout out to Todd, Tanner, and Conner. I don't have the authority to do it—but I genuinely believe Dana, the mom, should be made an honorary Eagle Scout as well!

Since you learned in the last book that I'm the freakin' Michael Phelps of Googling, I did some research. I found out only four percent of scouts ever make it to Eagle. The Malones have three of them. Great job, guys!

I started off with all of this scouting greatness because I rank at the bottom of the other 96 percent of America. In fact, I'm a CUB SCOUT DROPOUT. That says a lot about me, right?

As a kid, I had a great start in Cub Scouts. I loved the uniform, the people, and all of the early badges. The high point was when I won the Pumpkin Decorating Contest. At the time, I had no idea that I had already learned how to suck up to authority.

How did I do it? My Pumpkin Decorating Contest-winning design was a Cub Scout. Yep, I decorated my pumpkin to look like a Cub

Scout. It had a Cub Scout hat, a Cub Scout sash, and other parts of the uniform. It was an easy decoration. Why didn't anyone else think of it?

It was an amazing victory. I was at the top of the Cub Scout class. There were "future Eagle" whispers everywhere. Then, it all went to hell in a hand basket. Epic fails are mild compared to what I'm about to describe to you. It took me years of therapy and hundreds of Snickers bars to now be able to talk about it. Yes, I'm ready to tell you about...

PLAY SINISTER MUSIC IN YOUR MIND

The Pinewood Derby Fiasco.

Sometimes at sports events, you see fans of the home team mock star players on the other team and chant, "overrated." This didn't happen to me at the Pinewood Derby, but in my revisionist history, it now feels that way. Basically, I went from the top of the Cub Scout class to a Cub Scout has-been, all in the course of two measly Pinewood Derby races.

For starters, the Pinewood Derby car kit looks pretty innocent. It's this block of wood with some plastic wheels. You carve the block, paint it, and hammer the wheels on. Then, it is entered into this seemingly innocent Cub Scout race on this seemingly innocent Cub Scout track, so all the scouts can have some seemingly innocent fun. I had no idea how sinister this event really was—this was not included in the Cub Scout oath or the Cub Scout manual.

While I was sloppily hacking my block of wood into the shape of a jagged car with my trusty Cub Scout knife, there were teams of Cub Scout dads with engineering degrees and side deals with NASCAR carefully crafting my friends' cars. They hadn't cared about the Pumpkin Decorating Contest at all—they were all about this racing event. They scoffed at the ribbon I had won.

It was all a giant diversion. While I was playing with pumpkins, they had already built their Pinewood cars and were racing them in secret events in smoke-filled rooms, late at night, off the radar of the Boy Scouts of America.

And there I was, hammering on the little wheels to the badly carved wood block—each wheel more uneven than the one before it. I found some gaudy blue paint in our garage and glopped it all over my Pinewood project. For days after that, I ran it all over the house, making racing noises and inexplicably calling my car the "Mean Machine."

There was no doubt in my mind that I was going to win the Pinewood Derby. I worried about winning another ribbon and all of the extra attention that would come with it right after my big pumpkin victory. I practiced giving the Cub Scout handshake so it would be perfect when I accepted the Pinewood Derby award.

It could not have played out any more differently.

Far from professional in my automotive racing approach, I dangled my car by its wheels as I entered the school gym for the contest. Conversely, many of the other kids had special cases for their cars. In fact, their dads yelled at them if they even held the cases a little sideways. They sat quietly in their chairs as if they were holding a dangerous explosive device.

Me? I dashed all over the gym, making racing noises and running my car across walls, through stacks of chairs, and across the stage. I actually lost my car under the bleachers for about five minutes. When I fished it out with an old broom, it was so dusty that I had to rinse it with water in the drinking fountain and dry it off by wiping it on the pants of my uniform.

The Pinewood Derby was a double-elimination tournament. The Scoutmaster put up a poster board bracket to track all the races. We had several dozen cars in the competition. Nervous dads muttered curse words under their breath when they thought their first-round match was too difficult.

My first opponent was this kid named Craig who had one of the car-carrying cases. Craig's car was bright orange, shaved to look like a missile, and had probably been tested at Talladega. It shot out of the gate and beat my car by about half the distance of the track.

I was actually OK about it. Everybody was so enthralled with Craig's car that they didn't seem to notice the fact that my car really sucked. I retrieved my car after the race and began shaking off the loss.

I decided it would go faster if I pressed it really hard into my palm and kept revving the wheels like I was powering up a top to run across the floor. This was a horrible strategy. Each time I did it, the wheels became looser and looser.

Losing the first race meant I got to race in the loser's bracket for the second one. I was really happy to be matched up against this unpopular kid named Ben. Of course, I changed Ben's name for this story. It's not that I was very popular either; it's just that Ben ate a lot of Kleenex and rarely brushed his teeth.

His car? He had just nailed the wheels on the block of wood without bothering to carve it into the shape of a car. There was no paint. The wheels were at different angles. He had crudely scribbled his name in capital letters in magic marker on the top. So, it was the BEN CAR against my Mean Machine.

The races progressed until it was my time on the bracket to race again. I ran the car across my palm again. The nails on the wheels were now very loose. What's more, I think the four wheels of my car were pointing in four different directions. It was already clear that I would never become an engineer.

These two shameful cars were loaded into their respective starting gates. And, we were off... Well, Ben's car was off. It wobbled back and forth on the track hitting each of the walls as it squirmed along like a turtle.

The Mean Machine? When the gate opened, it tried to race, but one of the wheels caved in—followed by the other three. It dragged along for a second, and then came to a stop—on the incline of the track.

The Scoutmaster was trying to make light of it, but he commented that he had never seen one of these cars stop. He hadn't even thought it was possible until he saw it with his own eyes. I'm just glad there is no video of the race. In today's world, a video like that would break the Internet and millions of people would be laughing at me.

Even with the absence of a video, however, it was a miserable experience. Not only had I lost to Ben and been eliminated—I had created the worst Pinewood Derby car in scouting history.

This was not a kinder, gentler time. One dad became so frustrated with my racing ineptness that he yelled at me, "Just get away from the track, and get your car out of everybody's sight!" I've never seen that strategy in any parenting manual.

Tears welled up in my eyes. I hung my head and plotted my next move. I walked toward my car. AND THEN I RAN out the back door of the gym. Usain Bolt would have been proud of my pace. I ran all the way home and hid in my room. It was near the end of the school year, so my parents home-schooled me for the rest of the year.

No, that's not quite what happened. I did run, however, and I did catch a break. My dad was in the military and we moved away that summer. I was free from a life of never-ending Pinewood Derby failure ridicule. God bless the U.S. Army!

I never went back to scouting. I never even wondered what might have been if I had stayed.

Back to present day.

As I looked around at the Boy Scouts gathered for the Eagle celebration, I thought to myself—Scott, you are probably still the worst Pinewood Derby car builder in scouting history. This made me smile. I'm not sure why, but it somehow gave me closure.

Tweet me @mentalkickball if you are part of the 96% of the population that is not an Eagle Scout.

Hear the iTunes/Apple Music Version

GOOD FOLKS, BAD COACHING

(FOUR-YEAR-OLD SOCCER)

*S*ometimes in confrontational situations, you take the high road. Maybe Michelle Obama tells you to do it—maybe it is a little voice inside your head. Alas, this is not one of those situations.

Many of you may be involved in youth sports. I admit, I take that stuff way too seriously. In fact, I have a youth sports story where I behaved so badly that you may even feel sorry for me.

It starts innocently enough with me teaming up with my neighbor Todd to coach a soccer team for FOUR-YEAR-OLDS. Full disclosure —I have never played soccer. I can't name international leagues. If the subject comes up, I throw around Manchester, Chelsea, and the USA Women's National Team like I know what I'm talking about.

To me, soccer for four-year-olds looks like a big ball of jerseys on top of untied shoes, moving around a tiny field. There isn't exactly a lot of coaching to do. It's actually fresh-air daycare. The games are short. Players eat a lot of snacks and you constantly tell them to stay hydrated. The first order of business is to stock up on juice, water, and oranges.

The main challenge on game day is making sure your players

know which goal is theirs and which one belongs to the other team. You don't want the dreaded "own goal." To that end, we bought a plastic shark that was about two feet long because our team name was "the Sharks". We also got some Velcro strips. We were ready for our first game, or so we thought.

Being the home team, we Velcroed the plastic shark to the top of the other team's goal. Suddenly, the other coach, dressed in a replica World Cup uniform, marched over and angrily pulled our shark off their net.

"Hey, if that bugs you, we'll put it on our own net," I say as I walk up to him. I extend my hand for a handshake.

He blows me off.

"It's not going on either net," says Mr. I'm-Much-Better-Than-You Soccer Guy.

I say, "Look, they're four. One of the biggest challenges for them is remembering which goal is theirs. It will help your team, too."

The dude looks at me and says, "I once got invited to try out for the Random Country national team" (*I changed the name so that a whole country wouldn't be mad at me*). "Now," he says, "I have to deal with you putting a toy shark on the goal. That is bad coaching. You are obviously not a very good coach. What? Are you still going to have that on the goal when they are 17-year-olds?"

THIS IS FOUR YEAR OLD SOCCER

So, now I go from being a carefree coach to "I'd like to kick this guy's ass" in less than five seconds. That's jarring. I grit my teeth and say in my best Clint Eastwood teeth-clenched voice, "it's going on our net," after which I walk over and put it there.

THIS IS FOUR YEAR OLD SOCCER

The dude stomps away. About two minutes later, he walks back with another I'm-Better-Than-You Soccer Guy with a clipboard. Clipboard Guy identifies himself as the League Commissioner.

Commish says he's very worried because it's the first game of the season and the other coach has officially filed a protest. He says the other coach and his team feel uncomfortable and that's the worst thing that can happen in this league. Commish says there will be no use of sharks.

After a rant about tee ball, rails on youth bowling lanes, and flag football, I say I'm filing an official protest. Commish crossed his arms in disapproval and said I need to have a reason to file a protest. I say the other coach, his team's fans, and the Commish have made me feel uncomfortable.

So, we fill out another protest form. I ask for a copy of the form. Commish says he keeps the protest forms and the coaches do not receive a copy. So, I whip out my cellphone and take a picture of the form. I also squeeze off one of each of them and ask how to correctly spell each of their names. It's official—one game is to be played, there have been two pre-game protests, and three camera phone pictures.

THIS IS FOUR YEAR OLD SOCCER.

Commish then makes us shake hands. I ask if we need to hug as well. Commish comments he doesn't like my coaching style. I let him get about five seconds away before getting a little too close to the other coach and wagging my finger in his face.

In my best tough guy voice, I say, "I hope your team is good. If they're not, it's going to be open season all day. We'll see who's uncomfortable and who is a bad coach."

He thought for a moment and offered a lame reply. I think he said I would be a better fisherman than a coach since I have a toy shark.

THIS IS FOUR YEAR OLD SOCCER

Full disclosure, all of this would have set me off anyway, but my four-year-old son decided during warmup that he didn't want people watching him. He was on the sidelines with tears in his eyes. During practice, he was scoring goals from all over the field. Get him to the real game with a few people present and he came unglued.

That's perfectly understandable for a four-year-old, but didn't he realize we were playing for one of the most important prizes—male pride.

His teammate, Drew—we called him Droodle when he was four years old—had no such fear. With the tenacity of a World Cup pre-game talk, I pulled Droodle aside and told him to attack their goal early and often. I said I hoped he could hit double digits in goals.

Their coach started yelling pretty loudly at his players. They looked confused and in need of more snacks. I started pacing and sizing up the troops like General Patton. "Watch number four," I yelled. "He showed good speed during their warmup."

Two other fun pre-game notes for your reading pleasure—there are no goalies in 4-year-old soccer and the referee is just 10-years-old.

The game started, Droodle got the ball, dribbled right and BOOM —kicked it into their goal. We were up 1-0. The other team started the next action. Droodle stole the ball and kicked it right into the net. 2-0, baby!

THIS IS FOUR YEAR OLD SOCCER

The other coach made early substitutions, put his hands on his hips and kept yelling "defense" at the players coming off the field.

It's a running clock in four-year-old soccer. That means it doesn't stop for timeouts, or balls that go out of play, or anything else. They only play 12 minutes in a half. It goes by pretty quickly.

Despite the quick clock, Droodle scored TEN goals in the first half! Each one was better than the last. My fist was pumping like I was at a Metallica concert. I may have even been humming the song "Enter Sandman" each time Droodle scored.

The other team scored zero in the first half. They didn't even get a shot on net. It was glorious. I could hear the other coach at half-time barking at his player. He made them run a lap to think about all of their mistakes from the first half. Even though Droodle was grabbing every ball and scoring, I praised my team for playing together and showing great teamwork.

THIS IS FOUR YEAR OLD SOCCER

I pondered sitting Droodle out for a few minutes to start the second half. Then, I remembered the comments about bad coaching and 17-year-olds. Then, I took the high road and came to my senses.

No, that's not what happened. And, I know that's not what you wanted to happen either.

Yes, the goal became clear. Droodle needed to score 17 goals to exact the perfect revenge for the comment about sharks and 17-year olds. My testosterone made the call.

I'm pretty sure that's how the World Wars get started. Luckily on this day, there was no Archduke Franz Ferdinand and no access to any heavy artillery. My best weapons were Droodle and my camera phone.

The second half started with their best player making a move around one of our players. Then, Droodle stole the ball and pounded it into their net. We were on the board again. Droodle didn't raise his hands and celebrate. He was a quiet assassin out on the field. It was his very first soccer game, and he was taking to the sport like the proverbial fish to water.

Soon, Droodle was on the board again—and again—and still a couple more times. He had now reached fifteen goals. We were up 15-0, baby! The brass ring of 17 goals was in sight!

THIS IS FOUR YEAR OLD SOCCER

After a small scare when the other team kicked a ball that sailed wide of our goal, Droodle scored his 16th goal. To add to my poor sportsmanship, I had set a timer on my watch. I yelled, "Three minutes left. We need more goals, and we need to maintain this shutout. Keep feeding Droodle, he's got the rhythm of the game today."

After an almost tragic Own Goal, where one of our other players got confused and kicked it wide of our goal, we reached soccer nirvana. Droodle grabbed that rebound and smashed it into their goal for the 17th time!

I went into we-just-won-the freakin'-World Cup mode. I whooped and screamed and slapped hands with anybody within range. I then pulled Droodle out of the game, gave him a big hug, and told him this was a moment we were both going to remember for a long time. I said I hoped his teammates could keep up the shutout.

Guess what? We could! We ended up putting two more goals in the net for a final score of 19 to nothing. As time ran out, I stood there gripping our plastic shark and shaking it at the other coach.

"How do you like this protest!" I kept saying as he ignored me. He thought about it and then decided not to shake hands with me after the game. In fact, he pulled his team away.

They looked confused. It was tradition that both teams worked together after the game to make a tunnel of upraised hands that each player then ran through. It was a tunnel of one team today—our team that had won 19-0!

I calmed down some the rest of the season and even handled our one loss better than I did our most lopsided victory, the 19-0 game.

For the betterment of the entire planet, however, that's the last season I coached any soccer, especially...

FOUR YEAR OLD SOCCER.

Hear the iTunes/Apple Music Version

4

DON'T SUGAR COAT IT

(GIRL SCOUT COOKIES)

olks, I struggled to decide whether I should mention this problem, but it truly is a menace to society. Despite this, I have never seen a public service announcement that offers people help with this problem. In fact, it may be more addictive than Amazon Prime.

It used to be a situation where you had to pay cash, but that has changed. Recently, you could find me right in front of Walgreen's—checking both directions before handing over my credit card to get it swiped for more supply. Two days later, I was out there again.

It's harder for me because my neighbor is a dealer. She bragged that she has more than 1,200 boxes in her house. I know I'm addicted, but I also know the boxes are getting smaller, and the prices are getting higher.

It doesn't matter if you live in a large city or in a small town. Your community has this problem, and you can't win.

Yes, I'm talking about Girl Scout cookies.

I sometimes wake up in the middle of the night huddled up in a ball and shivering. I know the only cure is Thin Mints. Sometimes, I walk around work in a cold sweat. It's a good day if I open my file drawer and find Savannah Smiles or Peanut Butter Patties. At home, I found a partially eaten box of Thank You Berry Munch!

It's not the Russians or North Koreans that I worry about when my mind goes to dark places; it's the Girl Scout cookie factories. What if they go on strike? They could hold all of us hostage and take over America. Don't think they don't know that.

Google says we've bought as much as $785 million of Girl Scout cookies in a single year. According to Statistic Brain, 2.75 million girl scouts sell up to 28 different varieties of cookies.

Heaven help us all!

The future of America is not in the hands of the Republicans or the Democrats. It's not even in the hands of the military. Our future is going to be determined by the people that control the Girl Scout cookies.

You heard it here first!

Hear the iTunes/Apple Music Version

5

FUNNY SALES E-MAILS

J work in Marketing, so I'm the logical target of tons of sales calls and e-mails. The calls—I just screen them and hit delete.

E-mails? I'm always worried that sandwiched between the greatest deal on Earth and the erectile dysfunction spam, there's going to be an important company message that affects my career. So, I scan most of the e-mail headlines.

Even though I unsubscribe, block sender, alert every "no send" list, and cc the Pentagon, these sales e-mails come in by the dozen each day. So, I've learned to embrace them. I've even compiled all my favorite subject lines.

One of them said, "Here's the mascot solution you need." My creativity gets a little out of control sometimes. I pictured this joker painstakingly looking at every name on a list of thousands of e-mails. Then, he saw mine, smiled, and said, "Today is the day that Scott Murphy needs to pull the trigger on his mascot problem."

I almost replied to the guy to ask for some pricing, but I knew I would then dedicate way too much time to it. Does the head cost more if it's a weird shape? Does it come with clown shoes and regular shoes? How bad will it smell when you sweat? Is there a matching t-shirt cannon available?

I had to just hit delete. It was the best thing for everyone involved.

Another e-mail subject line said, "Who's handling your skywriting needs?"

I'm pretty sure that big companies like Google, Apple, Amazon, and Microsoft all have a skywriting guy on staff. Is my company out of touch? Or, is sky writing just a metaphor for reaching out to Millennials? Everybody wants to reach out to Millennials. Just as I was starting to brainstorm a new commuting game that mimics *Wheel of Fortune*, but with planes and sky writing, I had to take it down a notch. Again, for the welfare of everyone—I hit delete.

That same week, I actually got one with the subject line, "Do you know the extent to which you can raise morale by handing out personalized hockey pucks?" Sure, I like hockey, I like Wayne Gretzky, I once covered the Stanley Cup for radio, and I've recently been to Canada—but I decided to stay away.

Another one that gave me a weird feeling said, "Are you seriously breaking up with us?" It was from a vendor that we hadn't used in about three years. It gave me that same weird feeling in my stomach that many people get when a serious relationship talk begins.

I started humming Journey's song "Separate Ways"—*someday love will find you...* Then I hit delete and kept saying "It's not you, it's me."

You may be wondering what type of subject line has made me open one of these e-mails. A recent one involved Libya. Not my childhood crush—Olivia Newton-John—but the actual country of Libya.

It said we had won an award. We get a lot of these, but this one took the cake. Inside, it explained that our company won an award for being one of the most influential companies doing business in Libya.

What? We're a local credit union in Austin. It's as if some wickedly creative person said let's see how far we can go before companies stop buying these fake awards? Yes, I think sending it to my local credit union was a misfire.

But, if you send that bad boy to some overzealous high-tech company, they might go, "Hey, nobody else is getting awards in Libya, let's do this!" Also, I checked Wikipedia, and Libya is the 16th largest country in the world.

Another e-mail went beyond the award format and said we had been selected for the hall of fame. I opened that one. Pretty much any award that puts me into any type of hall of fame is probably worth a disproportionate amount of my attention. I just sat there for 15 minutes smiling, saying, "Thank you for putting me in the hall of fame," and looking like Will Ferrell discovering things in the movie *Elf*.

While some of the e-mail subject lines make me smile, some of them make me frown. I'm in charge of marketing at my work. I got a subject line that said, "Reduce staff. Reduce costs. Let us handle your marketing."

Double delete. Block sender. Alert FBI. What I really wanted was a "jolt sender with a double-strength cattle prod, disable sender's cell phone, and slash sender's tires" button. Thankfully, no such button exists at the time this book is being written.

This summer, I was on vacation and had the "I'm on vacation" e-mail message activated. During that week, the same person selling paper products sent me 31—yes, I counted them—you're welcome—31 messages about why their company was the best.

For just a second, I tried to picture the gang from Dunder Mifflin playing a prank on me. That crazy Jim Halpert and Pam Beesly! Later, I blocked the sender and deemed that 31 messages was a ridiculous move. Still, I may use somebody else's LinkedIn account sometime to see if I can see the picture of the person who sent me 31 messages.

Sending 31 is a calculated move, but they should know that "Back From Vacation Scott" has even lesser patience than Monday Scott. This version of Scott is only two spam mails away from being declared a grizzly bear.

A fun one I got the other day said, "Epic, shocking values. One item $2, two items $5." I opened it. Yep, this product is so good that there's going to be a shortage. So, they need to charge more per item if you plan on getting more than one of them.

It was a clever idea. I almost asked my company to change the prices of some of the things we sell. Sadly, I later figured out the head-line was a typo. Bummer. My reverse psychology theory had been reversed.

I didn't open it, but I smiled when I received, "Your current ink and toner provider is stealing you blind."

I was puzzled to read, "We'll teach you Spanish while your boss thinks you're working."

"Happy birthday, surprise gift inside," might have gotten me in the past, but I'm too jaded now.

Finally, I took a poll at work. Well, I stuck my head in the IT Department since they're the youngest folks in the building. I asked them what would make them open these e-mails. The results were fascinating.

They said Starbucks discount codes, pizza coupons, the word "zombie," the word "ninja," or anything related to *Game of Thrones* qualified. So, there you go. That's the secret to succeed if you're in the e-mail marketing game.

I have to run along now. I'm rolling out a new product for our company. It's a zombie/ninja checking account with fire-breathing dragons. You can earn rewards points for free pizza and Starbucks.

Hear the iTunes/Apple Music Version

6

BEER MAN

*S*ometimes in the workplace, an older employee mentors a younger employee, imparting wisdom and teaching them valuable life lessons. This is often a heartwarming tale that is suitable material for a major motion picture.

SOUND OF A RECORD NEEDLE SCRATCH

This is not that type of story. It's not even in the same universe.

At my first all-summer job, I was a busboy at a fish house restaurant that was in a mall in Virginia. I was 18 years old. There was a fellow busboy who was much older than me and who I liked to call "Beer Man." It was not a term of endearment.

He was not my boss, but the manager asked him to "show me the ropes." Need some perspective? Beer Man might have been worse at being a teacher than I was at being a Cub Scout. Now that I've provided you with a "wow" factor for this story, you can fully grasp it.

My fearless teacher never met a rule he didn't like to smash into little pieces. He would arrive late, take unannounced breaks, eat food left on diner's plates, pocket random items out of the kitchen, make unauthorized calls from the manager's office, and take beer home. And, that was just the first weekend.

Back to the beer. It was the way he took the beer home that made him the Beer Man.

Spoiler alert, he did it by using large, plastic mayonnaise containers.

So, you're thinking he acquired normal-sized mayo containers, washed them out, sanitized them, and then put beer in them. Not even close, Fun Stories Nation.

Let's dissect this whole process. The mayo we used came in huge plastic containers. I recently spent a ridiculous amount of time on Google researching mayonnaise. I'm surprised the Internet Police haven't knocked on my door, asking questions.

Sidebar, I will never pay full price for mayo again. I am getting Internet coupon offers from brands I didn't even know existed. Bottom line, I can only find one-gallon mayo containers on the Internet, but I know these were bigger. My head is huge and my imagination even larger, but I'm thinking, back in the day, the restaurant had three-gallon mayo containers.

At the end of the evening, once the restaurant closed and the beautiful people had gone home (the hostess, the manager and the waiters), we busboys would be in the back, spraying and cleaning stuff for a couple more hours.

Near the end of this process, the old cook would walk by and say, "Waste not, want not," to Beer Man. One of the few things I learned from Beer Man was that this was special fish house code. It was extremely different from that used by the military, but Beer Man would hear it and spring to attention as if he were suddenly in the Army.

PLAY SOME JAMES BOND MUSIC HERE FOR EXTRA FUN

Beer Man would then look at me very seriously, drop his voice to a whisper, and tell me I was in charge for the next few minutes. He said it like I was being handed the nuclear codes and there was going to be an oath of office ceremony. His spiel genuinely made me feel a little important.

Thinking he was James Bond, Beer Man would sneak into the kitchen and put the "empty" mayo container—with lots of mayo still on the inside walls—under the beer spout. The old cook would stand watch. You always needed a lookout if it was a good Fish House mission.

Beer Man would fill the whole mayo container and quietly screw on the big red container top. There would be mayo floating all around in the beer and cascading down the side where it had sloshed out while the top was put on. Suffice to say, it was a disgusting site.

Then, like Flounder carrying ten thousand marbles in the movie *Animal House*, Beer Man would scamper down the hall, give me a goofy thumps up, and trot out the back door. He'd slide the big container against the wall behind the big, smelly brown dumpster. He'd come back inside, give me another thumbs up, and then whistle loudly to signal to the cook that the mission had been completed.

Beer Man would then tell me he was in charge again. I never got to talk to any foreign leaders or propose any legislation. I did not even have franking privileges.

After we all clocked out, Beer Man would grab a trash bag and put it in his backpack. He and the old cook would exit the back door. He would make me stand there for a few minutes to ensure that the manager did not come outside.

I would count off three minutes (of unpaid time) on my watch and then head for the front exit. Outside, Beer Man and the old cook placed the mayo container in the trash bag and wandered off to the woods behind the mall for "Happy Hour." That's my teacher! Thankfully, I never got an invite to join the party. I once heard them say they liked to make a campfire when they drank the beer.

When all of this was happening, I frowned upon everything—as I probably should have done. Now, it seems to be a bit more charming. It's a sort of a Robin Hood-levels-the-minimum-wage-playing-field type of tale. It might just be my revisionist mind trying to justify the fact that I unwittingly helped them steal beer from the restaurant. It doesn't look that way when you're 18 years old.

For whatever reason, however, I think of these guys every time I see one of those Miller ads that talks about "The High Life." I think about them when Coors says they are "The Banquet Beer." I see their faces when I see Clydesdales on Budweiser ads. I'm not sure why.

The perfect ending to this story would be if Beer Man went back to school and became an actual teacher. Another good ending would be if Beer Man made millions of dollars by developing a microbrew using a mysterious secret ingredient (mayonnaise) that kept the public clamoring for more.

In actuality, I don't know what happened. I only worked with Beer Man that one summer. What I realize now, however, is that in his own dysfunctional way, Beer Man taught me some valuable life lessons— good and bad. Most important of these, don't judge people, and never pay full price for mayonnaise.

On a final note, for many years after this story, I switched from mayo to mustard on all of my sandwiches. But, with all of the coupons and discount codes now rolling in, I'm back, baby!

Hear the iTunes/Apple Music Version

7

UNLEASH YOUR OPINION

*T*rending topic alert! I'm seeing more and more of this on Instagram, Twitter, Snapchat, and Facebook. It's become one of the major issues of the day. You need to do your research and educate yourself to form a meaningful opinion on the subject. People are going to ask you about it. Your co-workers may alter their opinions of you based on what you say. Preparedness is the best way for you to handle this delicate situation. You need to be ready!

The important topic? Where do you stand on dressing up dogs in outfits? Is it fun? Is it wacky? Is it sinister? Does it make you a better person? What does your dog think about it?

I was eating lunch the other day and Spider-Dog walks by. The owner smiled like he had just won the lottery. If they put me in charge of marketing the next superhero blockbuster, I would hire hundreds of people to walk dogs in superhero costumes all around New York and Los Angeles.

I wonder if they make rock band t-shirts for dogs? Our dog Curly would look great in one of those! It would make our daily walks even more fun. Bottom line, there are dogs everywhere—and the opportunities to make products for them are endless.

I googled some interesting statistics about dogs to share with you.

We own 78 million dogs in the United States. In fact, 44% of American households have a dog. That's a lot of potential outfits.

I know Taylor Swift is a cat person, but I can't believe the Kardashians haven't come out with a clothing line for dogs. Why are there no dogs on the runway during Fashion Week? You heard it here first. Kate Upton, please take the lead on this project. You, Justin, and your dog Harley need to start a clothing line for dogs. That would be fun!

Folks living on the West Coast like dogs the most. 81% of them say they prefer dogs as pets. According to the American Kennel Club, the ten most popular names for female dogs are:

1. Bella
2. Lucy
3. Daisy
4. Lola
5. Luna
6. Molly
7. Sadie
8. Sophie
9. Bailey
10. Maggie

The ten most popular names for male dogs are:

1. Max
2. Charlie
3. Buddy
4. Cooper
5. Jack
6. Rocky
7. Bear
8. Duke
9. Toby
10. Tucker

Rover found that 53% of dog owners have named their dog after a TV character, book character, or celebrity. Here are 15 unique names people give their dogs according to the American Kennel Club:

1. Atticus
2. Aurora
3. Broderick
4. Copernicus
5. Einstein
6. Figaro
7. Gatsby
8. Keats
9. Lennon
10. Midnight
11. Phineas
12. Picasso
13. Prince
14. Sherlock
15. Willow

Have a good dog outfit picture? Post it to any of the Mental Kickball social media sites and let's start some additional fun.

Hear the iTunes/Apple Music Version

GEORGE CLOONEY TIME

*L*ife comes with a never-ending supply of questions. Your car is a great place to think about many of them. Here's an important one you need to address right now. Folks, this is serious stuff. Your social status may be on the line. At the very least, it's about family pride and tradition. Memories are there for the taking.

Of course, I'm talking about bobble heads.

I know they give them away at baseball games, but now there are companies that make personalized bobble heads. My co-worker got one for his birthday, and honestly, it looks terrible. I didn't even know such a thing existed. Did I miss an important text thread? Is Amazon to blame?

If you're a dad, your family has probably run out of gift ideas for you for Christmas. Then, they see an ad on YouTube and realize it's the perfect opportunity to make a personalized bobble head—of you. And, yes, it's going to look as bad as your mind is imagining it.

You need to act—right now. Let everybody in your house know that you need to be involved if they ever decide to make a bobble head of you. A bobble head should never be a surprise gift.

It sounds easy to have a bobble head made, but it's not. There are so many variables to consider. What would you be wearing? Is it still in style? Should you be wearing shoes? Of course, you want that. Don't let them show you with bare feet. You are not Fred Flintstone. You also don't want to be shown with any chest hair sticking out of your shirt. That's so barbaric.

The questions are nearly endless. Would you be playing a sport? Is it a cool sport? Is there a drink in your hand? Would your bobble head look cool in sunglasses? Would they consider that appearing on a bobble head usually adds 20 pounds, so they need to make your bobble head look at least 30 pounds lighter?

See, it's not an easy situation. Get it right. Upon completion, they'll display your bobble head right by the front door so everybody that enters the house sees it. Other than a nuclear disaster, the Kardashians getting cancelled, or losing the TV remote for an extended period of time—there is nothing worse than having a bad bobble head made of you.

My best advice is to execute a pre-emptive strike. Contact the bobble head company. Offer to pay them twice the price. All they need to do is use the George Clooney mold to make your bobble head. It's the perfect plan!

Despite having already given you the perfect plan, I know you are busy. You might not act quickly enough, and your family will get a bobble head made without your knowledge. You need to open it and act quickly.

For our friends in cold weather climates, there is an easy fix. Take the present. Walk closer to the fireplace. Pretend to trip over anything that's near the fireplace and drop the present into the fire. Even if they fish it out and it gets a little burned, it will still be better for you than it would have been before.

For our friends that do not live in cold weather climates, but have a dog; put that sucker right in the dog's mouth. Of course, don't harm the dog, but make sure the dog does some serious damage to the bobble head. Again, a damaged bobble head is far better than the normal ugly bobble head.

Another idea for our warm-weather friends that own a pool is to slip and throw it into the pool. Improvise if your climate and gift occasion are different than what we have listed here. Remember, it always starts with faking some type of fall.

Final note, develop a secret "they're making a bobble head of you" phrase with your male neighbors. This will help you warn each other if you think there's some unauthorized bobble head activity happening.

I suggest using the secret phrase, "Does that guy that looks like Chandler Bing still work at your office?" If anybody on your block hears it, they know it's George Clooney time!

Hear the iTunes/Apple Music Version

9

CEREAL MASCOT HALL OF FAME

I'd like to make a confession. Call me crazy, but I don't like to eat cereal unless it has a cartoon mascot.

Case in point, I'm watching the NBA playoffs and see an ad for Slam Duncan O's. This is built around the retired San Antonio Spurs legend, Tim Duncan. I love cereal, I love the Spurs, and I love Tim Duncan, but I want no part of Slam Duncan O's.

Why? This cereal has broken my cardinal rule of cereal consumption—it does not have a cartoon mascot. Of course, the high volume of sugar helps as well, but the cartoon mascot is what seals the deal for me.

Tony the Tiger? He's my all-time favorite cereal cartoon mascot. In fact, Tony the Tiger is cooler than 90% of the real people I know. Play the "Tony the Tiger Game" in your office. Watch co-workers go by and think, "Is Bob cooler than Tony the Tiger? Jill is gregarious, but is she better than Tony the Tiger?" Tweet us on @mentalkickball and tell us how many people in your office are cooler than Tony the Tiger.

Here's a quick cereal mascot quiz. What's the name of that crazy bird that is crazy for Cocoa Puffs? Is it Billy? Is it Crazy Jay? Is it something else?

GAME SHOW CLOCK EXPIRES

The correct answer is something else entirely. His name is Sonny. FYI, I look exactly like Sonny at 5 PM on Fridays!

There are lots of great cartoon mascots for cereals. We need a Cereal Mascot Hall of Fame. Wouldn't that be fun to visit? Let us know on the Fun Stories Facebook page why your town would be the ideal place to build this mascot museum.

Getting back to the hall of fame candidates, what about Toucan Sam? Yep, he's a hall of famer. He follows his nose. I love those Fruit Loops. No arguments here, he's a first ballot hall of famer.

Snap, Crackle, and Pop of Rice Krispies—they're kind of weird, but they have done just enough to be Hall of Fame worthy. That's the yard stick we can use. If they are not at least as good as Snap, Crackle, or Pop, they are not going into our Cereal Mascot Hall of Fame.

Cap'n Crunch? Yeppers! Hall of fame. He's a freakin' classic that people would pay money to see in the museum.

The Dig 'Em Frog? Now that's a cool mascot. Hall of Fame! He used to be all about Sugar Smacks, but now it's Honey Smacks.

I also remember when several other cereals used to have sugar in their name, before the government decided we were having too much fun at breakfast. I'm looking at you Sugar Frosted Flakes. Tony the Tiger—he's Teflon. He never got any heat in that whole sugar name scandal. But let's not allow any sugar affiliations to turn any potential hall of fame mascots into Pete Rose.

I love the monster mascots: Count Chocula, Franken Berry, Boo Berry—love, love, love! They are all members of the Hall of Fame. But sometimes, they try to throw Fruit Brute in there as well. No, sir. They've started and stopped that cereal so much, I can't keep track of it. No Hall of Fame for you, Fruit Brute. The same goes for Fruity Yummy Mummy. Is that one really a part of this group? Absolutely no hall.

I'm also saying NO to the Bigg Mixx animals and any Alpha Bits mascot. Aren't there like ten of them?

Lucky the Leprechaun and his Lucky Charms are a cereal main-stay. Hall of Fame. The Trix Rabbit—you can't talk about cereal mascots without giving props to the Rabbit. Trix are for kids—irrespective of their age—AND the Hall of Fame was made for the Trix Rabbit.

But it's not all sunshine, roses, and unicorns in the cereal game. There are mascots I don't like—that will never make the Hall—and they are usually the healthier alternatives.

Quaker Oats? That smiling Quaker guy—even in cartoon form—is not really a mascot; he's just creepy. No Hall for you! The Rooster on Corn Flakes? No Hall. Why would you go with that stuff and not choose Tony the Tiger. Don't play the health card on me. No Hall.

Sometimes even being a Hall of Fame mascot can't get a cereal flavor off the ground. There used to be Cap'n Crunch's Choco Donuts, the crunchy chocolate flavored cereal. You know the American Dental Association freaked out over that one. There was also a Cap'n Crunch's Deep Sea Crunch with these colorful fish, but we weren't buying it.

Kellogg's, the breakfast behemoth, once had C-3PO's, a crunchy new force at breakfast. They even had Star Wars trading cards inside. How did that one miss? You just know their marketing team was so fired.

Ralston once offered Donkey Kong Junior cereal. It was "wild with fruit flavor!" I guess we were not wild about it. Maybe it took time away from actually playing Donkey King. All I know is that when I think about it, it makes me want to jump over barrels in video games.

Post once offered Smurf Magic Berries. There was even a Smurf Chase Game on the box! More marketing people were let go after that one.

Even GI Joe once had a cereal. I wonder if you got Kung Fu grip if you ate it. My Mental Kickball senses tell me I would have loved to have played that "Kung Fu Fighting" song while eating this cereal. Even if the cereal is gone now, somebody please make a YouTube video of GI Joe dancing with Barbie to "Kung Fun Fighting." That would be incredible!

Since we're so random, I can't let you go without mentioning that Mr. T once had a cereal. I never ate it, but the cereal box had letters in it. They were all the letter "T." I pity the poor kids (Mr. T voice) that grew up with a limited vocabulary because they ate too much Mr. T cereal. Also, my Beavis and Butthead radar is going off. Fifth Grade Scott would have giggled like Beavis and Butthead, spread out two of the "T" letters of the cereal and then put his index finger between them to make the letter "I." I don't know what's worse, the fact that Fifth Grade Scott would have done that over and over, or the fact that present day Scott instantly sees that opportunity and throws Fifth Grade Scott under the bus.

Remember, it's not just breakfast, it's a chance to put cereal mascots in the hall of fame. Choose wisely. Final note, I personally challenge you to make your next breakfast hall-of-fame worthy.

Hear the iTunes/Apple Music Version

TAYLOR SWIFT CLARIFICATION

*A*t this point, I want to clear up any confusion. Despite her global social media domination, you do not get a medium boost or a high boost on the Taylor Swift section of the Ticketmaster website when you visit *Fun Stories* sites. I'm glad I had a chance to clear that up.

MONDAY SCOTT HATES FRIDAY
SCOTT

*M*entioning Monday Scott in the e-mails chapter sent my mind racing. I'm sure your company constantly tells you to work hard and be consistent. Sure, that's sounds great to say, but does your boss realize we're all at least seven different people?

Let's analyze this situation—it might help all of us be better employees, or at least more informed employees. *Your employee performance may vary.*

For starters, I've never seen the movie *Split*—you know, the one about the guy with some-20 different personalities—but I think all of us have some of that going on.

In fact, I think there exist 7 different Scott Murphys—one for each day of the week. And some of them—I'm looking at you Monday Scott—like to work against the others.

Listen to the following examples. You may be dealing with a similar situation.

Let's start with Monday Scott. Well, he protests the entire day, starting from the moment his alarm goes off. Monday Scott is in a fog. He may have stayed up too late watching his DVR, or he may have just jacked up his sleep schedule.

Monday Scott is no less than a caveman. He drools a lot and stares at the computer screen for hours. Monday Scott should never attempt to undertake any meaningful projects, or he might just bring the whole company crashing down.

Sometimes Monday Scott is ready for lunch and it's only 9 am. Sidebar, as I write this, the earliest I've ever stepped out for lunch is 10 am. What's the earliest you've ever taken your lunch break on a regular work day? Back to Monday Scott. Monday Scott is like a boxer who is just trying to hang on till the final bell and not get knocked out.

When Tuesday Scott arrives at work, he sometimes thinks Monday Scott may not have been in the office at all. If Monday Scott did some things, it might take all the way until the arrival of Thursday Scott to get those things all straightened out.

Tuesday Scott has a better disposition than Monday Scott—unless it's Tuesday Scott coming in after a three-day-weekend. Then, Tuesday Scott is even worse than Monday Scott. Overall, Tuesday Scott usually manages to make some progress. He's not real friendly, but Tuesday Scott gets by if he gets enough snacks.

Wednesday Scott? Wednesday Scott likes to say "Hump Day" a lot. He has a lot more energy than Tuesday Scott or Monday Scott. Wednesday Scott is optimistic about all of the company's projects.

Even though it's only Wednesday, he starts the whole "it's almost Friday" conversation in the office. People hate hearing that on Wednesday. Wednesday Scott makes progress and likes to point out on Wednesday afternoon that more than half of the week is over.

Watch out for Thursday Scott. He's one day away from the end of the work week and he knows it. Thursday Scott used to go all-in at Happy Hour on Thursday nights before he became a family man. He still thinks about those feelings fondly.

Nowadays, he only he goes all-in emptying his change drawer to get sodas and snacks so that he still feels like he is getting a Happy Hour. Make sure you locate Thursday Scott late in the day so you can experience his epic countdown to Friday.

Friday Scott? He's a fan favorite! Friday Scott comes into the office with a great attitude and high-fives people everywhere. Sometimes, he brings tacos. That doesn't happen too often, but in his mind, it's a regular thing.

Friday Scott constantly tells people "Happy Friday, man" and does this little half salute. People enjoy that. I wonder how he thought of that one. If you ever interview to become a cruise director on a ship, go in there with Friday Scott's energy. Yes, Scott does Friday like a boss!

Saturday Scott? Saturday Scott is pretty chill unless somebody messes with his sleep pattern and/or forgets to turn off the regular morning alarm.

Don't make any appointments with him early on Saturday morning, or it's worse than poking Monday Scott with a stick. Saturday Scott has been waiting all week to sleep in on Saturday.

Saturday Scott's bed is like a phone charger, and he has run the battery all the way down to zero. Later in the day, Saturday Scott can be a fun guy. He might even barbecue for you—or at least point you in the direction of a good barbecue restaurant.

Sunday Scott? Sunday Scott is a classic underachiever. He's one day away from having to go back to work and he knows it. All he wants to do is sit around in his underwear, watching sports and eating pizza.

Even though he doesn't have to work on Sunday, he's still too lazy to take care of the chores that need completing. He loves to mess with Monday Scott. He knows Monday Scott has it bad anyway, so Sunday Scott does things like not gassing up the car and not going to the grocery store. Sunday Scott likes to smile and say he'd hate to be Monday Scott.

There you have it. There are seven days in a week and seven different versions of you. Multiply that by the current world population of 7.6 billion, factor in that the world is currently adding 150,000 people per day, and you may want to hit the snooze button more often. An alternate idea is to declare a mental health day, get several more hours of sleep, and enjoy more *Fun Stories* books. Make Sunday Scott proud!

Hear the iTunes/Apple Music Version

CRAB LEGS ROMEO GAME SHOW

a few weeks into my job at the fish house, I got promoted. Beer Man was really peeved about it. He had worked there for many years, but he had never even been interviewed to be a waiter.

The moment of my promotion went like this. Our highest-ranking manager comes walking by one day and says "Scott, you're in college, right?"

"Yep," I said.

"Well, you probably ought to be a waiter now," said the manager.

If I had known an interview situation was going down that day, I would have studied the periodic table and memorized the names of most of the Presidents. I would have made more eye contact, given a firmer handshake, and revised my resume. Sometimes, however, it is better if a business takes a "pull the band-aid off quickly" type of approach. No worries, just a promotion—that's not a bad thing.

Speaking of Presidents, Beer Man once asked me which President I liked best. It was so random, and he was so not one for educational conversations. In fact, he bragged about having liberated himself from school at the age of 16.

I replied saying that Harry S. Truman was my favorite because I was born in Missouri (shout-out to the St. Louis Cardinals). Beer Man pulls out his wallet and waves around a one hundred dollar bill. "I think it's obvious who the best President was," he says—Benjamin Franklin. I just smiled and felt like it would have made me a bad person if I had corrected him.

After extremely minimal training, I was declared an official fish house waiter. We had this all-you-can-eat seafood buffet on the weekends. We were told that each plate we sold would mean better revenue for the restaurant and a much better tip opportunity for us. It cost $17, but it had crab legs, scallops, flounder, and four types of shrimp. There was no time limit. Some people arrived early in the evening and ate for several hours.

The second night of my waiter career, a disheveled man came in, claiming he loved crab legs and was looking for an adventure. "Just call me 'Mr. Crab Legs,'" he chuckled. Before I could even pitch him the buffet, he said he wanted to order two of them. I looked around and didn't see anybody else.

Mr. Crab Legs? Adventure?

I explained to Mr. Crab Legs that it was an all-you-can-eat buffet. He said, "Yup, I'll take two."

I explained that he could go back over and over and basically camp there until closing time. He grew impatient and said to just bring him two plates. I tried a different approach, telling him that the buffet cost $17 and I would then have to charge him $34.

"That's what I want, already"—Mr. Crab Legs said.

So, I brought him the two plates. He put one in front of him, and the other across from him.

For about 45 minutes, Mr. Crab Legs ate. After each plate he finished, he would get up, go to the buffet, fill up the plate again, but not immediately return to his seat. Mr. Crab Legs would wander into other sections of the restaurant like he was lost. He'd then return to his table—all the while leaving the empty plate just sitting across him.

An hour into his meal, Mr. Crab Legs ordered three beers from me. I'm thinking, "One guy, two plates—now three beers?" I went to the bar, got the beers, and brought them to his table.

"Game on," said Mr. Crag Legs. "You are in charge now," he added.

I was really confused. I was in charge? Was he going to try and fill mayo jars with beer?

"Can't you see what's happening?" Mr. Crab Legs said.

I could not see. Bottom line, I was scared that adventure meant he was going to chug the beer and try to leave without paying—and more importantly, leave without giving me a tip.

Mr. Crab Legs offered more details. He said he was trying to find a woman. He thought he could land one by offering an all-you-can-eat meal upgrade to an attractive woman eating a lesser-priced meal. Hence, the empty plate. I thought that was a fairly clever approach. I love game shows!

He said the strategy wasn't working. Side note, if Mr. Crab Legs had combed his hair, dressed up a little bit, and worn cologne, it might have helped with this whole process.

Mr. Crab Legs went on to say that I was the second-best looking guy in the restaurant and he needed my assistance. Second best? Was this a compliment?

Mr. Crab Legs said I should carefully look over all the women in the restaurant, rank them, and offer a beer to the three best matches for him. It was kind of a *Love Connection* meets *The Dating Game* meets *Let's Make a Deal* type of hybrid game-show experience.

Mr. Crab Legs said the back story is important in these types of situations. He asked me to tell the women that he was a shy Hollywood Director who was scouting talent for his next movie. He also asked me to tell them that he didn't want a lot of attention. He was just looking to have a fun night with a nice, church-going woman.

Mr. Crab Legs said he wasn't religious, but women that went to church were usually better in bed. Boy, was I copiously making page after page of mental notes!

Then, he really amped up the game show. He offered me $20 on top of the regular tip if I got a woman to have dinner with him.

Mr. Crab Legs probably had a van outside with lots of lotion and went by the nickname of "Buffalo Bill," but it was an offer a college student could not refuse. Conversely, to give me more of a performance incentive, he said he would cut my tip in half if I could not find a woman to have dinner with him. What? Really? Don't ever do this to your waiter.

I didn't know his age. Anybody above 25 looked 50 to me back then. I'm guessing now that he was about 35. For better or for worse, the game show adventure had started.

I knew he wasn't from Hollywood, but I still felt a little giddy about posing as a scout for a Hollywood Director. I quickly spotted a hottie two sections over who was showing a little cleavage. I refilled her hushpuppies, got a weird look from her real waiter, and gave her a free beer. Just then, her husband returned from the bathroom. Stupid me, I should have checked for a ring first. Besides, this woman was way out of his league. Strike one. Game shows are harder than they look.

I played a lot of sports in high school. This was a similar situation. I gave myself a pep talk on what it took to win this game. For starters, I needed to use my resources better, come up with a bigger idea, and maximize this opportunity. I decided that my best play was to find a group of women that had already been drinking. They would be in the appropriate state of mind and more likely to jump at the offer. I could present the idea to the entire group, not lose any of the remaining free beers, and move on if there were no takers. Then, I chickened out of that idea. I wasn't brave enough to ask one girl out, much less attempt to pitch a date with a stranger to a whole group of unknown women.

Semi-defeated, I shared my game show dilemma with the bartender. He was a 50ish (I think) guy that might have some sage wisdom. Before he could offer any advice, the sluttiest waitress in the place—the kind your mother warns you about—chimed in because she had overheard me telling my story to the bartender.

"I'll do it," she said, "but it's going to cost you. This is a big favor." I felt like I was making a deal with the mob. She had worked the day shift and was about to clock out. She was very tired, but she was willing to do me this favor if I covered two of her future day shifts. It seemed like a high price to pay for giving her the chance at a couple of free beers and a free $17 buffet, but I took the deal.

FYI, the day shift had terrible tips, so she really maximized her opportunity. The game of life is often a far better teacher than a book or an adult in the classroom.

I feel bad calling her the "slutty waitress," but several guys in the place (not Beer Man) had been with her, and she didn't deny it when they told the sordid stories. She had also told me a couple times before that I "looked good in those pants." To use The Joker's quote from the *Batman* movie, I was "dancing with the devil in the pale moonlight."

The slutty waitress took the two beers, went to Mr. Crab Legs' table, and they hit it off famously. She ate free food for more than two hours, and he laughed like a teenager at everything she said.

I think I won the Crab Legs Romeo Game Show. In fact, I ended up getting a $40 tip! All of my years of watching *The Price Is Right* may have helped.

I know, I know. You want more details about the two of them. Well, late in the game, Mr. Crab Legs asked her to go home with him. She said she was tired from working all day, but she would like to thank him in a special way. She dragged him into the women's restroom—I'll tell you more about that restroom later—and gave him some special service.

She bragged about it for weeks. It's no wonder she had the reputation that she did around the fish house. Everyone was amazed that she had met a Hollywood Director and he was going to give her a role in his next movie. There is a song by Jamie O'Neal called "There Is No Arizona" in which a man promises a woman that he'll call her later and then give her a new and better life in Arizona. This is the same type of thing. I mention this because I often play content-appropriate songs while writing these stories. That was what I was listening to when I wrote the last part of this story.

Truth be told, she was over-the-moon happy for several weeks before she realized she didn't even know his name. Still, she thought maybe he would show up again or call the restaurant and ask about her. As you might imagine, that never happened.

At the end of the story, there was no movie role, there was no

Hollywood, and he was no Hollywood Director. In all fairness, she was not the "nice girl" he was seeking, and neither was she a church-goer. TV game shows seem like so much fun, but real-life game shows can be very complicated. But, it's an imperfect world, and this was an imperfect adventure. During this adventure, however, she got a lot of free beer and crab legs, he got some special service, and I got forty bucks. So I guess it was a win-win for everybody.

Hear the iTunes/Apple Music Version

13

OFF THE MENU CRAZY (ULTIMATE WAITRESS REVENGE)

*W*ARNING: DO NOT READ THIS STORY IF YOU ARE CLOSE TO HAVING YOUR NEXT MEAL OR SNACK.

There's one girl I will always remember from the fish house. I don't even remember her real name because all the workers just called her "Crazy." She didn't work in our mall restaurant very long, but she created memories for many of us that will last a lifetime.

I know you go to fast food places or sit-down restaurants and sometimes receive less than the desirable service and/or food quality. Then, you wonder whether your waiter will mess with your food if you complain. Based on my restaurant experience, I have the answer —YES!!

This is the part where my former co-worker nicknamed Crazy takes the stage. Crazy was about 25 years old, barely 5 feet tall, black hair, fit, cute but street-tough cute. If you squinted, she looked a little like Pat Benatar.

According to actual facts and stories I heard from my co-workers, Crazy had a couple of kids, a couple of failed marriages, and a couple of restraining orders. I may have added an extra restraining order just to add more synergy in the story.

Remember, sometimes, I take liberties with these stories, and sometimes, I take the whole damn statue.

I first met Crazy when I was a bus boy. My work area, where I sprayed the dishes and ran them through the drying machine, was in the back of the fish house opposite a huge walk-in cooler. There were many things in the cooler, including chocolate pudding.

Crazy loved chocolate pudding. I don't know why she did, but love is an understatement. Almost every shift I worked with her, she would tell me to be the lookout. Notice there are a lot of lookouts in these fish house stories? She'd go into the cooler for a few minutes and eat as much pudding as possible.

I'm now thinking this would make for a great game show on Nickelodeon that features lots of food eating games. The restaurant kept the pudding in little glass dishes on a big tray inside the walk-in. She'd exit the cooler and hand me 4–5 of those empty glass dishes to clean.

Crazy would thank me for being a lookout and laugh a devilish laugh. Sometimes, she would seductively wiggle her tongue in and out of her mouth with pudding on it to surprise me. It definitely got my teenage attention. I think she was auditioning me to be husband number three, but I was far too stupid to realize it.

Crazy was always nice to me, but I heard cooks and other waiters say very crazy things about Crazy. Supposedly, they saw her doing the following:

- Pop pills in the hall
- Give money to people that stopped by the restaurant
- Smoke joints in the bathroom—which might explain the pudding
- Randomly stab things in the kitchen with the biggest knives

They said she openly talked about wanting to kill her first ex-husband, probably with a knife. She said she was cool with her second ex-husband. I don't know how much of this was real and how much was urban legend. I was too preoccupied watching and thinking about her sticking her tongue in and out of her mouth with pudding on it.

One day, this cranky man came in and was not happy that he had been seated in Crazy's section. He immediately started ordering Crazy around. There was history. No, she hadn't been married to him. He was this grouchy old man she had waited on several times before. He had not tipped her on any of those occasions.

We were a fish house, but he ordered a Salisbury Steak. It wasn't on the menu. Because of that, Crazy had never served Salisbury Steak at our fish house. He insisted it was a menu item.

Crazy asked the manager and found out we did offer it. It had been a menu item in years past. It was basically the leftover steak from the day before, served with a gruesome gravy we made with flour and grease drippings. The old man belittled Crazy for not knowing about it.

Crazy was having a good day and took all of this early guff in stride. Soon, she got the off-menu Salisbury Steak meal from the cook and took it to the grumpy old man. Crazy placed it down and started to walk away. Like a drill instructor, he told Crazy she had not been dismissed yet.

He tested it with his finger and asked her to take it back because it wasn't hot enough. He yelled loudly that he was one of the restaurant's best customers and always got this waitress, who was one of the worst ones he had ever seen.

Crazy was still surprisingly calm as she asked the cook to heat it some more. A couple minutes later, Crazy took the Salisbury Steak back out to the man. He tested it with his finger again and gave an even ruder response than the first time. His face was red, his arms waving. He screamed that Crazy was incompetent. He said he didn't know how she could function as a human being. He wanted his food hotter. He then spelled the word hotter, letter by letter to make sure she understood him. He asked if she was on furlough from the state pen. That was the only way he could figure that she could be holding on to her job. All of this over Salisbury Steak that wasn't even on the menu.

Now, this is the part of the story where Crazy lived up to her name.

Crazy took the food and stomped back to the kitchen. I had never believed the knife stories, but she grabbed a big knife and started stabbing the steak like she had done this before. She chopped it into tiny pieces and yelled. I was equal parts frightened and aroused. The plate cracked. She slid the meal onto another plate and then smashed the broken plate against the wall. Her face was blank. She was there but she wasn't there. I was now more parts frightened and less parts aroused.

Then, Crazy acted out your worst fears. Piece by little piece, she crammed almost all of the chopped steak into her mouth. She made an awful face and CHEWED and CHEWED and CHEWED the old man's Salisbury Steak. She then dribbled it out of her mouth, piece by piece, back on the plate. Her payback process had only just begun.

Next, Crazy made gurgling noises with her mouth and then proceeded to SPIT and SPIT and SPIT more on the plate. After that, she ladled on more gravy and put it in the microwave for several minutes. The best way I can describe what it looked like when it came out of the microwave is to ask you to picture smashed up road kill, add gravy, and imagine lots of smoke coming out from it.

But, wait. There's more. After the microwave, she bent over his mashed potatoes, covered one nostril, blew out snot—and repeated the process with the other nostril. Then, she added more gravy. Finally, she licked the top of his dinner roll. Now, it was ready.

Practically every worker in the restaurant watched as Crazy calmly walked back out and put the plate down on his table. Old-yelling-guy touched it with his finger and almost burned himself. He took a little bite and happily proclaimed "This is the way I like it. This meal is the best kept secret in this whole town!"

If he only knew.

For weeks, all of us would point at food on the plates and say, "This meal is the best kept secret in this whole town!"

Did Crazy finally get a tip that night? No. Old guy stiffed her again. She quit working there a few weeks later. The rumor was that she had run off to Las Vegas with a local drummer to get married again. I just thank God it wasn't me. During that naïve time of my life, her feminine wiles coupled with her seductive chocolate pudding games could have probably made me follow her anywhere.

Crazy comes to mind any time I get frustrated with restaurant food. Instead of getting mad, I picture Crazy chomping away on that Salisbury Steak and spitting it out piece by piece. I see her covering her nostrils and booger-bombing the mashed potatoes. I then smile and accept whatever weirdness the server of the restaurant has sent my way.

I suggest you do the same. But, if you do decide to make a stand, don't ever do it with any order that includes gravy.

Hear the iTunes/Apple Music Version

14

THE NAKED FOOTBALL PLAYER MEETS THE MARCHING BAND (BIG BOBBY)

*H*ope your day is going well. Even if it's a little iffy, I want to share a quick story that is a textbook example of a guy that has had a really bad day. The hope is that by hearing the story, you'll relax and say, "You know what, my day is OK." For this story, we climb into the Way Back Machine and go to Kansas.

It's the beginning of high school football season. Picture me, a 10th grader with poofy hair and braces—but the story is not about me. I was only a reluctant observer. I won't even disclose the high school name since the story gets very embarrassing for one poor guy. We'll just call the high school *Random Kansas High School.*

RKHS didn't have freshmen, so all of the pranks got played on the sophomores. It was not a kinder, gentler world, and the Seniors got away with a lot more hazing in those days. I got off pretty easy. That meant having some powder put in my helmet a few times and, on one occasion, getting deep heat rub put in my jock. In comparison to the treatment some of the others received, that was pretty pedestrian stuff.

We'll call the focus of our story BIG BOBBY. Big Bobby was not very athletic. He was noticeably overweight, had a low interest in football, and struggled with all of the exercises and running. He appeared out of place on the football field. He once said he was only there to try and lose a few pounds and please his dad. The coaches were sure they could make him into a powerful offensive tackle. On the practice field, he struggled to block anybody. He just wasn't fast enough. The better older players on defense would go flying by him, slap his helmet, and yell, "Woo—weeee, Big Bobby can't block!" often.

Off the field, Big Bobby had these big glasses and a virtual Three Stooges haircut. Fashion was not his middle name. He had crushes on several girls, but he would stand too close to them and creep them out when he tried to talk to them. They would always get uncomfortable and find excuses to go away.

On the upside, Big Bobby was great at math. He always won the competitions we had in math class. He also won the pizza eating contest the football team held one day after practice. In short, he had a huge appetite for math as well as most types of food.

Big Bobby always had a huge lunch that he carried around in a big brown paper grocery bag—not your normal little lunch bag. The older guys soon figured that out, and he would win their approval by offering them cupcakes and bags of chips. It looked like he was successfully bonding with some of the Seniors by sharing his lunches.

One day, however, he shared too much—information. He told them he mainly played football because the best-looking girls always wanted to date the football players. Amused, they asked him if he could sex any girl...yep, that was a cool term at the time—*"Yeah, I think I could sex that hottie."* Anyway, they asked Big Bobby which girl he would pick.

Big Bobby said he would like to sex this girl named Judy that played flute in the band. Of course, I changed Judy's name for this story. I also used the name Judy so that we can call her JUDY FLUTIE. Doesn't that make it more fun and accessible? You know this is a going to be a train wreck for Big Bobby, but you can't even imagine where we are going with this cautionary tale.

Most days while we practiced football after school, the band would practice in the school parking lot. There were even football field markings painted on the parking lot so they could properly practice their halftime shows.

Football involves a lot of practice, but more days than not, the band was still practicing when football practice ended. The football team liked to goof on them by running through their formation when the players were cutting through the parking lot and heading to the locker room. On more than one occasion, Big Bobby would stand close to Judy Flutie and admire her. It even seemed that Judy would appreciate the attention.

Following Big Bobby's lunch confession that he would like to sex Judy Flutie, the older guys paid more attention to this subject. They watched him watching her, cackling and whispering to each other. Something was brewing, and it was not going to be good.

Big Bobby finally entered the locker room, stripped, and entered the shower. As I was checking items in my locker for foreign substances, I saw a bunch of the Seniors head to the shower—still in their uniforms. This was really not going to be good. I did what any sophomore should have done. I walked to the far end of the locker room and got the hell away from whatever mayhem was about to take place.

Next thing I know, I hear all of this high-pitched yelling and screaming. A whole group of Senior guys came out of the shower room... and they had a completely wet, completely buck naked Big Bobby, completely hoisted in the air. As he yelled and screamed, they carried him out the door and chanted, "Judy, Judy, Judy!"

Once again, they barged into the band formation. This time, they marched right up to Judy Flutie and tossed her naked admirer at her feet. He covered himself as best he could, looked around in horror, and started to run. The guys tried for a brief second to herd Judy toward him, but the band teacher yelled over the megaphone for them to leave or face lots of detention. They chose to leave.

Next, the Seniors inside held the door shut and made sure Big Bobby had to walk through the school to get back to the locker room. This meant a lot more exposure to surprised students and teachers. As he walked through the coaches' offices to get back to the locker room, they seemed OK with it. Nowadays, there would be a million lawsuits over the incident.

On a brighter note, the prank seemed to change Big Bobby's status on the football team and in the school. The Seniors mostly left him alone after it. It seems they felt like he had now properly paid his dues. Even better than that for Bobby, his Full Monty walk created lots of stories and rumors. All of them were very positive for Bobby.

Word quickly spread that he had lived up to his Big Bobby nickname during his naked march and proven to be very well endowed. He got asked to the Sadie Hawkins dance by another girl in the band. I'm almost positive, however, that he never had the chance to sex Judy Flutie. The prank had created too much pressure for 10th graders, or any other grade for that matter. Sadly, she asked one of the football pranksters to the Sadie Hawkins dance.

My family moved to my dad's next military assignment before the school year ended, so I don't know what happened to Big Bobby in his upperclassman days at RKHS.

Here's how I hope it ended.

I sincerely hope Big Bobby got a great education, a great job, and became the boss of some of those incorrigible RKHS guys. I hope he has a big house, a great family, and despite his math expertise, he has trouble counting all of the money he has made. Throw in a cool dog and a white picket fence, or a large security gate, and the vision is complete.

Using this story, you can compare most of your so-called bad days to the day he had, and they'll probably not seem as bad. If that's the case, raise your glass and toast Big Bobby.

Let's all toast him together right now. "To Big Bobby! Hear, hear!"

Hear the iTunes/Apple Music Version

15

DAD PRANKS (DRINKING WHISKEY AND CHASING FAST WOMEN)

J'm proud to be a raconteur. In fact, I come from a long line of storytellers.

Here's the proof.

As you already know, my dad was in the Army when I was growing up. He would travel a lot and sometimes bring back interesting stories. He especially liked to tell silly stories to my grandmother (his mother-in-law) because she was gullible in a very endearing way.

She would ask him about his "army missions," and he would tell her funny stories and call her "Lucy." I think he used it as a term of endearment for her as well as a tip of the cap to the great comedic genius of Lucille Ball.

Setting the story, I'm five-years-old and playing with toys on "Lucy's" floor. My dad was about to go off on an army training trip. My grandma asked him where he was going and whether it was some type of special mission.

My dad didn't miss a beat and said, "Lucy, it's a real special mission. It's a very important one. I'm going to be out there helping our country by drinking whiskey and chasing fast women."

That was pure old-school humor. She laughed. He laughed. I kept playing with my toys. They thought me to be none the wiser. I especially like how it was fast women—not just women. We Murphys enjoy adjectives.

So, Dad goes off on his "special mission," and the next day, my mom drops me off at Sunday school. My Sunday school teacher was an older lady named Mrs. Scheperle and was a really good friend of my grandma. Mrs. Scheperle called me "Scotty."

She said, "Scotty, I only saw your mom when you got dropped off. Is your dad out of town again for the army?"

"Yes" I said and offered nothing else.

"I'll bet it is a secret mission," she offered with enthusiasm.

Hearing the word "mission" clicked five-year-old Scotty into a different gear. "Yes, it is a special mission" I said.

She said he is probably keeping our country safe and learning how to stop bad guys. "No," I said matter-of-factly. "He's drinking whiskey and chasing fast women." She acted like that was normal conversation, and I kept coloring Jesus pictures.

Later, at church, Mrs. Scheperle smiled and told my grandma the story. Then, my grandma told my mom. My mom didn't think it was as funny as everybody else. Me? It was all in the course of a normal Scotty week.

Hear the iTunes/Apple Music Version

16

PAYING MY DUES

a little earlier in the book, I started the dialogue about my first job at the fish house by telling you about the Beer Man. We later met my co-worker, Crazy. Finally, I want you to meet the assistant manager, Helga. Of course, Helga is not her real name.

Helga interviewed me for my original bus boy job at the fish house. I dressed for success. Thanks, Mom! I actually wore a suit and tie to interview for the bus boy job. Helga offered me the job right in the middle of the interview. That should have served as a warning. Sure, I probably interviewed well, but I think I got the job as soon as Helga saw my tie clip and the military shine my dad helped put on my shoes.

Helga was a round woman, somewhere in her 60s, with cat eye glasses, beehive hair, and bright red lipstick, looking like she walked right out of a Gary Larson cartoon for *The Far Side*. She had worked in the mall for more than 20 years, and it had earned her a little host stand at the front of the restaurant by the lobster tank. It was her own little bizarre world.

Helga would hum and talk to nobody in particular. One of her favorite pastimes was naming the lobsters. She would wonder aloud whether "Big Claws" or "Mrs. Claws" would get eaten that day. She once held a moment of silence when "Pointy Claws" was chosen from the tank. It seemed all of the lobsters had the last name "Claws." Helga said they were all on death row and she was the warden. If they crossed her, she would serve them up to the next customer.

Helga would compare their plight to our human world. She'd say the lobsters might be safer than us. She would cackle that any of us could get taken out by a bus, or shot dead in the mall parking lot just as easily as one of the lobsters could get eaten that day. It was her own Maya Angelou "caged bird" logic. For some reason, however, my interpretation of it made me never want to ride the bus.

What's worse is Helga was an inappropriate kisser before we knew inappropriate kissers were inappropriate. She wanted to close-hug you and KISS YOU ON THE LIPS when she saw you. Yes, it was just as bad as you're imagining it to be. In today's work world, she would last about five minutes, but this was an everyday thing back then.

To finish the picture, Helga loved wine. She kept a bottle under the counter. She'd frequently sneak it out and take a big slug—right out of the bottle. It made her slur her words and confused the customers that often busted her taking a swig. Helga would also sneak-smoke inside the restaurant—sometimes right at her station.

Despite Helga's unique managerial skillset and my unconventional training from Beer Man, things moved along pretty well in the bus boy world for the first week. I could spray the hell out of the dishes and was way faster at my work than Beer Man. Productivity was way up at our mall restaurant.

Just when I was getting comfortable, Helga and Beer Man played their favorite new employee prank on me. Again, nowadays it would be Lawsuit City, but back then, it was great fun for them.

It started by Beer Man asking me if I "had paid my union dues." I mentioned that I had not heard about that in the interview. Beer Man asked me if I had been hired right on the spot when the interview finished. I confirmed that was the case.

"Oh, man. You're in the union and you don't even know it," he said. "Helga will be coming to collect your dues any time now."

I inquired about the cost of the dues, and he just chuckled. He said

I was naïve and didn't realize that the dues were not money. They were about taking care of a "special project" for Helga. He laughed a hee-haw kind of donkey laugh and soon implied that it meant Helga would be asking to spend private time with me.

I suddenly felt like I was the new guy in a prison. How would I handle the special project? About two hours later, Helga came to the back and said I needed to go with her to take care of a special project.

Holy crap, it was happening.

Helga led me down the hall by the women's restroom and said she wanted to show me something. I pondered excuses in my head if she tried to put the moves on me in there. I also wondered if I would lose my "man card" if I just started yelling for help to save me from this old lady.

"What's the matter?" she said. "Your voice is shaky. Don't you want to help me?"

I just looked at her with wider eyes as Helga flung the women's restroom door open. Then it happened. It's not what you are thinking.

I smelled it before I saw it. Someone (was it Beer Man?) had left a big, steaming pile of poop right in the middle of the floor in the women's bathroom. It wasn't really steaming, but as you know, we Murphys love us some adjectives. I was actually relieved. I could figure out how to handle that project.

"It had to be a man," she said, and tried not to laugh.

She then went into fake Angela Lansbury crime-solving mode. She said, "Let's review this case. No woman would poop right on the restroom floor. We know that much." She concluded by calling it one of the biggest mysteries she had seen in months. That had been the last time they had hired a new employee.

"This mystery may never be solved" she said.

With that, she left me to clean it up. She slapped me on the butt as she left. When I saw her later, I confirmed that the project was complete.

"Welcome to the union, honey" she said. "Your dues are all paid up."

Working your first job can sometimes teach you a lot about

people, especially the way they act. In this instance, it was an "I will never do that to another human being" type of lesson.

Later in the year, when I worked at the fish house during Christmas break from college, Helga reached new levels at the Christmas party. She wore a low-cut dress and close-danced with several of the cooks. She got louder and louder and kept yelling, "All of ya need to be payin' your dues!"

Your boss is looking pretty OK right about now, eh?

Hear the iTunes/Apple Music Version

17

CLOWN COMMUTER AWARD
(BEWARE OF LANE BEGGARS)

*T*he Clown Commuter Award game is supposed to be fun, but it makes me angry to launch into this one. It's a nuisance to the entire commuting game. It happened to me again just last week. I'm talking about the freakin' guy that gets out of his car at the stoplight and walks over to ask the driver of the car in the other lane to let him in. What the hell? You, sir, are a Clown Commuter Award winner.

First off, do not get out of your car. Ever. It's a cardinal rule of driving. Pretend the highway is engulfed in flames, or it's shark-infested water and you are not watching Shark Week. Stay inside your vehicle, already.

We are all dealing with enough baggage from our day. We're dealing with road construction and endless turmoil on the highway. We're worried about what North Korea might be thinking—or not thinking. We do not want to deal with people walking out of their cars trying to barter for lanes as if they are trying to sell us Amway.

If you're not man enough to grab the lane during normal traffic maneuvering—sack up, go through the intersection, and contemplate an alternate strategy. Your GPS will know what to do. Do ANYTHING but get out of your car and beg other motorists to let you into the lane. That's almost the equivalent of accepting a trophy just for participating in a sport. You didn't earn it, Clown Commuter!

I'd almost rather drink expired milk than watch someone get out of their car and bargain for a lane. Well, not really, but it illustrates how much I hate lane beggars.

Sidebar, it was a funny thing in high school when we would walk to a fast food restaurant and place an order at the drive thru without the benefit of a car. That's cute—it's not begging for a lane. Evidently, that is still a thing.

I was in Houston last summer and actually saw a fast food place with a sign that said, "must have vehicle to use drive thru." I'll bet Chick-fil-A will still give you the "my pleasure" treatment—even if you go through the drive-thru without a vehicle.

But back to Mr. Get-Out-Of-Your-Car-And-Lobby-For-The-Lane. You are a menace. You are one of the major reasons why our video games have gotten so violent.

You are the winner of a Clown Commuter Award. In fact, I'd like to offer you the award, then break it into a dozen pieces as you are reaching for it. After that, I'd like to take your lane and watch the confused look on your face.

A final thought on the topic—men are notorious for not wanting to ask for directions if they are lost. This makes it even more ponderous as to why these troglodyte men will get out of their cars and beg for a lane.

If you have an answer, please pass it along on one of the social media sites. We need your help!

Hear the iTunes/Apple Music Version

18

MURPHY'S LAW

*H*ave you heard of Murphy's Law? It says, "Anything that can go wrong, will go wrong."

It even applies to me when I'm driving. So, it's Monday and I'm leaving work late. I'm tired and my car's AC is on the fritz. To top it all off, I'm somehow out of car snacks. Just when I think it can't get any worse, BAM—I'm rear-ended at the stoplight.

Because I'm in "pity party for Scott" Monday mode, I react slowly. I look up just in time to see the car that hit me go flying around me, run the red light, and turn left. Hey, I watched at least the first four of those *Fast and Furious* movies, so I decide to give chase.

I am not Vin Diesel. It's not even close. Don't ever try this at home.

At the time, I was thinking that I could at least get close enough to them to get their license plate number. So, I ran the red light and turned left. Full disclosure, I am neither fast nor furious.

I did catch up a little bit. In the distance, I could see the car that hit me. The guy mashed the brakes and did a Tokyo Drift turn. That move is not in my driving repertoire. It made me consider quitting the chase, but Murphy's Law made me keep going.

After I made a far less impressive turn, I lost sight of the rear-ender. What I did see, however, is a police car about a block down the street on the left. I pulled in behind it. I popped out of my car and dashed toward the driver.

In my mind, there was nothing more important in the world than my problem. I was ready to ask if they could radio all of the other police cars in the city to track down the car that rear-ended me. Perhaps, they could even alert the FBI.

Again, don't try this at home.

It's a big surprise to me now that the police officers stayed fairly calm. They just firmly asked what I wanted. I say, "I've been rear-ended, and I need your help in apprehending the subject."

Their police radio is going a mile a minute. I guess I looked like a member of the "10 Least Wanted" list. Sidebar, why can't I look dangerous? What does it take to look dangerous?

They quickly grew impatient with me. They yelled for me to get in the back of the police car.

Get in?

Confused, I climb in the car. The driver-side cop tells me to put on a police helmet and get as low to the floor as possible. Oh crap, what is going on here? The helmet feels weird on my head—then I realize I put it on backwards.

On the police radio, I heard raised voices and scuffling. I find out later, the guys in my car were the outside part of a drug bust taking place in the nearby apartments.

While I hunkered on the backseat floor, the two of them debated what to do with me. They wondered if I was in more danger here, or if I tried to make it to my car. Tried to make it to my car? Go to hell, Murphy's Law!

They responded to the radio saying that they were ready to join the fray if they received the word. Then, they whispered something about me and handcuffs. My eyes were big, and I would have been scared of dying, but I'd forgotten to use the bathroom before leaving work. So, I was more worried about peeing my pants.

I tried to suppress the negativity by humming that "Bad Boys, Bad Boys—what cha' gonna do" theme song from the TV show *Cops* in my mind.

Was it in my mind? One of the policemen said I seriously needed to stop humming.

Thankfully, they got the "all clear" message about 20 minutes later, and they said I was safe. I sat up to tell my tale. Only, my mind was so jumbled that I couldn't remember anything about the car that rear-ended me. I was useless.

I did think of traffic cameras, but they checked and there were not any at that intersection. There was nothing they could do for me.

MURPHY'S LAW SUCKS.

As I exited the car feeling stupid, they pointed out that I had forgotten to return the police helmet. I tried to squeeze off a selfie with the police car to commemorate the experience, but as Murphy's Law would have it, my battery had run dry.

Hear the iTunes/Apple Music Version

NAME TAGS

OK, one more quick fish house story before I go. Have you ever had to wear a name tag at work? For no particular reason, I think it's funny to point out that your name tag is extremely important while you work for the company. If you lose it, you could even get suspended or fired. Later, when you leave the job, the same name tag means absolutely nothing.

I have several old work name tags in a drawer. They trigger a lot of memories. I enjoy the TV show *Superstore*. It is a fun running gag on the show that America Ferrera's character, Amy, wears a different name tag every week. It's interesting to look out for the different name tag each week.

As you've read here, there were a lot of odd things about the fish house, but near the top of the list was the wait staff name tags. For example, a girl that had "Felicia" on her name tag was not named Felicia at all. And it was not an Amy-from-Superstore type of thing.

It turns out that she had been given Felicia as a "good waitress name" by one of the male managers. Soon, I learned that almost all of the other girls had "waitress names." This was supposedly to help them earn better tips. I never saw that in any Marketing books, but lots of celebrities use different names.

For me, it made it seem like I was working in a secret spy world where everybody was a double agent. I was not very good at talking to girls to begin with, but this made it doubly awkward.

In later years, I wondered whether some of the male managers spent a lot of time at strip clubs and then used those names for the fake waitress names. No male waiter ever got assigned a "waiter name."

To this day when I think about the women that worked there, I wonder what their real names were. I'll probably never get the answers I seek. I should probably stop wasting so much time thinking about it.

I'd like to sincerely thank you for reading this book. It means the world to me. As Cronin says, "Stick together, keep each other warm, and always keep ridin' the storm out!"

And when the work day is over, remember what McConaughey says, "Alright, alright alright!"

Thanks again for reading this book!

Hear the iTunes/Apple Music Version

ABOUT THE AUTHOR

~

R. Scott Murphy looks at the world in fun, sometimes twisted, ways. He is the madcap mind behind the *Fun Stories* series of humorous eBooks, albums, and audiobooks. Part storyteller, part game-show host, part DJ, and part madcap tour guide, the award-winning author resides in Austin, Texas, with his wife, two sons, and a rescue dog named "Curly."

Murphy holds a master's degree from the University of Missouri School of Journalism and has taught advertising at the University of Texas. An experienced TV and radio personality, stadium announcer, advertising writer, TV game-show producer, and sports producer, he uses his many experiences as inspiration for *Fun Stories*.

Murphy is a four-time winner of the "Late Show with David Letterman" Top 10 List Contest, plus a Remi Award winner for script writing. The first three eBooks in the *Fun Stories* series reached #1 on Amazon Humor. Numerous audio versions of Murphy's stories have charted on the iTunes Comedy Songs rankings. "Chick-fil-A Makes Me Feel Like Leonardo DiCaprio," "I'm the Freakin' Michael Phelps of Googling," and "Shamelessly Suggestive City Names" all hit #1. Check out Apple Music, Amazon, and Spotify for Murphy's complete audio catalogue.

Murphy enjoys playing loud music, learning air guitar, watching sports, reviewing all the oddball shows he records on his DVRs, and collecting vinyl and CD versions of the classic *American Top 40* radio show with Casey Kasem.

YOUR VOICE COUNTS

YOUR VOICE COUNTS

I'm an independent author. Your review can make a huge difference. If you enjoyed this book, please consider giving it an honest review on Amazon. Thank you for your consideration.

Review this book

See the next book in the series

R. Scott Murphy's Amazon Author Site

POST-GAME SHOW

~

The credits are rolling, but if you keep turning the pages, you might just find some more fun!

YOU'RE IN THE BONUS ROUND!

BONUS MATERIAL

You found the Bonus Material! I like to call this "Ferris Bueller Time." It's the bonus information after the credits roll. For me, it's an integral part of the *Fun Stories* formula.

This time around, I want to share some additional information about Girl Scout cookies. Do you know which type of cookie is the most popular? Turn the page to find out. What's more, I have a second round of bonus material for you that shares a lot more crazy dog names!

BONUS MATERIAL I

DON'T SUGAR COAT IT
(GIRL SCOUT COOKIES)

BONUS INFORMATION

According to Business Insider, these are the five top-selling types of Girl Scout cookies:

5. Shortbread (Trefoils)
4. Peanut Butter Sandwiches (Do-si-dos)
3. Peanut Butter Patties (Tagalongs)
2. Samoas (Caramel deLites)
1. Thin Mints

It's interesting to follow up on the national ranking with a listing of the most popular Girl Scout cookies in each state. This information is courtesy of Insider.

Thin Mints are the most popular type of Girl Scout cookies in almost half the states in our country:

- Alaska
- Arkansas
- Arizona
- California
- Delaware
- Hawaii
- Idaho
- Illinois
- Indiana
- Maryland
- Michigan
- Minnesota
- Nebraska
- New Hampshire
- Nevada
- Ohio
- Oklahoma
- Oregon
- Rhode Island
- South Dakota
- Tennessee
- Utah
- Virginia
- West Virginia

Samoas reign supreme in 18 states:

- Colorado
- Florida
- Georgia
- Iowa
- Kansas
- Kentucky
- Louisiana

- Massachusetts
- Maine
- Missouri
- North Carolina
- North Dakota
- New Jersey
- New Mexico
- New York
- Pennsylvania
- Texas
- Washington

Tagalongs are the favorite in six states, plus the District of Columbia:

- Alabama
- Connecticut
- Washington D.C.
- Mississippi
- Montana
- South Carolina
- Wisconsin

Do-si-dos top the list in two states:

- Vermont
- Wyoming

What's my favorite type of Girl Scout cookie? Thin Mints are my favorite, but they were not listed as the favorite in the state where I live, Texas. What happened, y'all?

If you don't agree with the results from your state, eat more of your favorite type next time around!

I'd also love to hear from the Thin Mint Nation on any of the Mental Kickball social media sites. Specifically, do you keep them in the refrigerator? For me, that makes them twice as tasty. Also, do you dunk your Thin Mints in milk? I do not do that. I just rapidly toss them in my mouth like I'm loading a machine gun.

BONUS MATERIAL II

UNLEASH YOUR OPINION

BONUS INFORMATION

Since I'm the Freakin' Michael Phelps of Googling, I'm still surfing for outrageous dog names even though the "Unleash Your Opinion" story was completed a long time ago. Thank goodness for bonus features and social media. Sometimes, a topic is like the Hotel California for me—I can check out any time I like, but I can never leave.

Anyway, here's a fun list of 25 more outrageous names for dogs. These came from *Dogtime*. Thank you!

- Amarillo
- Atlantis
- Barack
- Bluegrass
- Chevalier
- Dubya
- Elton

- Ferrari
- Flush
- Greely
- Honey Blue
- Isuzu
- King Arthur
- Kong
- Lolita
- Mercedes
- Obama
- Oreo
- Pandora
- Socrates
- Thor
- Tsunami
- Utopia
- Valentino
- Ziggy

SPECIAL GUEST APPEARANCE

Here's a picture of our family's beloved dog, Curly. She's always ready to help make some more Fun Stories. Watch for her contributions to my weekly Fun Stories Universe newsletter.

BOX SET ALERT

Fun Stories Box Set #1 (5 books). This release contains Fun Stories Books 1-4, plus a giant bonus book, Fun Stories Almanac. Enjoy 14 never-before-released stories and nearly 1,000 pages of humorous short stories! Read it free on Kindle Unlimited.

R. Scott Murphy's Amazon Author Site

FUN STORIES UNIVERSE

GET MORE FUN AND FREE STUFF

Keep the fun going! Get updates, free stuff, and early info about Scott's latest projects by reading his Fun Stories Universe weekly newsletters. You can get a free Fun Pack when you subscribe at www. mentalkickball.com. It may even make you say, "Alright, alright, alright!"

BOOKS BY R. SCOTT MURPHY

Fun Stories For Your Drive To Work

Fun Stories For Your Drive Home

Fun Stories: Random City Limits

Fun Stories: Searching For More Cowbell

Fun Stories Greatest Hits

Fun Stories Box Set (Books 1-5)

Ducks on the Pond

AUDIOBOOKS BY R. SCOTT MURPHY

Fun Stories For Your Drive To Work

Fun Stories For Your Drive Home

Fun Stories: Random City Limits

ALBUMS BY R. SCOTT MURPHY

Fun Stories For Your Drive To Work

Fun Stories For Your Drive Home

Fun Stories: Random City Limits

iTUNES COMEDY SINGLES BY R. SCOTT MURPHY

Chick-fil-A Makes Me Feel Like Leonardo DiCaprio

I'm the Freakin' Michael Phelps of Googling

Shamefully Suggestive City Names

Happy Friday (Mr. Pee Man)

Cub Scout Dropout

George Clooney Time

Good Folks, Bad Coaching (Four-Year-Old Soccer)

Chick-fil-A: The Rest of the Leonardo DiCaprio Story

THANK YOU FOR READING AND LISTENING!

ACKNOWLEDGEMENTS

Thank you to all of the good folks who were kind enough to offer free images on Pixabay for use by indie artists such as myself. Please review their creative work on Pixabay and consider hiring them for your next project.

Alright, Alright, Alright! (OpenClipart-Vectors)

Cub Scout Dropout (Clker-Free-Vector-Images)

Good Folks, Bad Coaching (luvmybry)

Don't Sugar Coat It (OpenClipart-Vectors)

Funny Sales E-mails (Geralt)

Beer Man (alles)

Unleash Your Opinion (skeeze)

ACKNOWLEDGEMENTS

George Clooney Time (YS-Park)

Cereal Mascot Hall of Fame (Jambulboy)

Taylor Swift Clarification (OpenClipart-Vectors)

Monday Scott Hates Friday Scott (sferrario1968)

Crab Legs Romeo Game Show (Clker-Free-Vector-Images)

Off The Menu Crazy (OpenClipart-Vectors)

The Naked Football Player Meets the Marching Band (Clker-Free-Vector-Images)

Dad Pranks (OpenClipart-Vectors)

Paying My Dues (OpenClipart-Vectors)

Clown Commuter Award (Meridy)

Murphy's Law (aitoff)

Name Tags (edwardpye)

About the Author (Jenny Murphy)

Reviewers Needed (TKaucic)

Post-Game Show (RyanMcGuire)

Bonus Round (Vivs4e)

Bonus I (OpenClipart-Vectors)

Bonus II (skeeze)

Special Guest Appearance (Griffin Murphy)

This Again? (GraphicMama-team)

Photo Credits (OpenClipart-Vectors)

Fun Stories Wants You (Tumisu)

THANKS AGAIN!

YOU ARE MUCH APPRECIATED

If you enjoyed this book, please consider giving it an honest review on Amazon. Thank you for your consideration.

Review this book

See the next book in the series

R. Scott Murphy's Amazon Author Site

Made in the USA
San Bernardino, CA
13 December 2019